HarperCollins
Entertainment
An Imprint of HarperCollins*Publishers*

COLUMBIA PICTURES PRESENTS A MARVEL ENTERPRISES/LAURA ZISKIN PRODUCTION
TOBEY MAGUIRE "SPIDER-MAN 2" KIRSTEN DUNST JAMES FRANCO ALFRED MOLINA ROSEMARY HARRIS DONNA MURPHY
MUSIC BY DANNY ELFMAN PRODUCERS STAN LEE KEVIN FEIGE EXECUTIVE PRODUCER JOSEPH M. CARACCIOLO BASED ON THE MARVEL COMIC BOOK BY STAN LEE AND STEVE DITKO
SCREEN STORY BY ALFRED GOUGH & MILES MILLAR AND MICHAEL CHABON SCREENPLAY BY ALVIN SARGENT PRODUCED BY LAURA ZISKIN AVI ARAD DIRECTED BY SAM RAIMI

MARVEL   SPIDER-MAN CHARACTER ™ & © 2004 MARVEL CHARACTERS, INC. ALL RIGHTS RESERVED.   sony.com/Spider-Man   DISTRIBUTED BY COLUMBIA TRISTAR FILM DISTRIBUTORS INTERNATIONAL

Spider-Man 2: Spider-Man Versus Doc Ock

Spider-Man and all related characters: ™ and © 2004 Marvel Characters, Inc.

Spider-Man 2, the movie: © 2004 Columbia Pictures Industries, Inc.

All Rights Reserved.

First published in the USA by HarperFestival in 2004

First published in Great Britain by HarperCollins*Entertainment* in 2004

HarperCollins*Entertainment* is an imprint of HarperCollins Publishers Ltd,

77-85 Fulham Palace Road, Hammersmith, London W6 8JB

1 3 5 7 9 8 6 4 2

ISBN 0-00-717820-4

Printed and bound by Scotprint

Conditions of sale

www.harpercollinschildrensbooks.co.uk

www.sony.com/Spider-Man

SPIDER-MAN 2™

Spider-Man Versus Doc Ock

Adaptation by Acton Figueroa

Illustrated by Jesus Redondo, Ivan Vasquez,

and the Thompson Bros.

Based on the Motion Picture

Screenplay by Alvin Sargent

Screen Story by Alfred Gough & Miles Millar and Michael Chabon

Based on the Marvel Comic Book by Stan Lee and Steve Ditko

HarperCollins
Entertainment
An imprint of HarperCollins Publishers

Sometimes I do not know what is harder: being a hero or being a student.

When I am Spider-Man, I help others.

But sometimes I need help, too.

Like today—I am late for class again.

I do not want to be late for this class.

Dr. Connors is the professor.

I like him a lot.

I wish I could tell him why I am always late, but no one can know that I am Spider-Man.

After I run into him, Dr. Connors
reminds me that I have to write
a big paper for his class.

I am going to interview a scientist
named Dr. Octavius.

He is performing a very dangerous
experiment today.

I know all about danger.

Helping mankind is my

after-school job.

As my Uncle Ben said,

"With great power comes great

responsibility."

Helping people feels good.

I think that Uncle Ben

would be proud of me.

I do not get nervous when I am
saving people.

I do not have time.

I just go to work.

This is the fun part.

My job as a photographer is fun, too.

Working at the newspaper means
I always get the news before
anyone else.

Doc Ock?

That is a funny name.

It sounds a little like Dr. Octavius.

I hope that nothing went wrong with
his experiment.

I better take my paycheck to the bank now.

Yikes!

I am not the only one with
superpowers at the bank.

That is not the right way to make a withdrawal!

I think it is time for Spider-Man to

help these people . . .

. . . before Doc Ock takes off
with all the cash!

He is ready for a fight and so am I.

Let's go!

You missed me, Doc Ock!

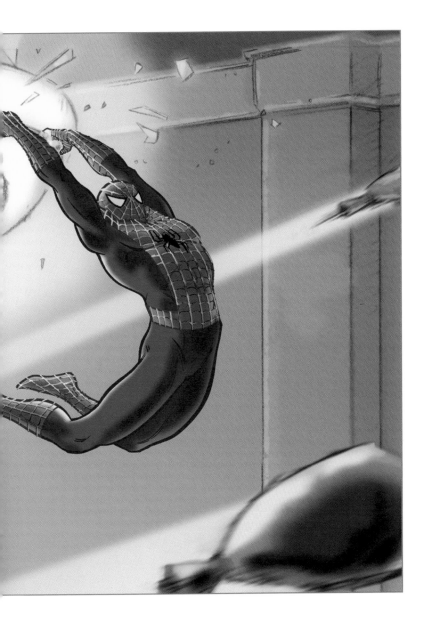

Ready or not, Doc Ock, here I come!

Fighting someone with four extra

limbs is not easy.

My spider-strength comes in
handy at times like this.

Be careful on the way down!

Doc Ock is gone for now,

but he will be back.

And I will be waiting for him,

protecting the people of this city.

That is what a hero does.